You can't betray your best friend and learn to sing at the same
time

Kim Hiorthøy

nordisk books

Published by Nordisk Books, 2016
www.nordiskbooks.com

Translated from 'Du kan ikke svikte din
beste venn og bli god til å synge samtidig,'
copyright © 2002 Forlaget Oktober A/S.

Translated by Kim Hiorthøy & Duncan J. Lewis

Cover illustration by Kim Hiorthøy
Cover design © Nice to meet you

Printed in Great Britain by Clays Ltd, St Ives plc

A CIP catalogue record for this book is
available from the British Library

ISBN 9780995485211

You can't betray your best friend and learn to sing at the same time

One morning, right after breakfast, the doorbell rang. I went to open, and then I started to hesitate. It rang again a few times and then it stopped. I did not move. Only about half an hour later did I open the door, and then there was no one there.

It was only October, but it had become cold and miserable and damp. I didn't have any money, nor a proper job really, but just before the weekend I was given a minor commission by my brother in law to draw sheep. It was for the Farmers' Collective, for which he worked, but I couldn't get the animals to look right. I sat and drew and looked out at the rain and mainly felt like giving up. But the rent was due, it had been for a while, and this was no time to be evicted. Better to draw sheep than return to the post office, had they been willing to give me the job back. There was something about the head, where it starts to become fleece, that I couldn't get to work. It was hard to tell it was sheep. I called Erika and asked her what I should do. The mysterious is the most beautiful thing we can experience, she said. I repeated this, a few days later, when I stood in my brother in law's small office and showed the drawing to him.

Late one afternoon while I sat alone and let my thoughts wander, the doorbell rang. I opened and it was Henriette. She was naked and it looked like she had been running. Hi, I said. Hi, she said. Can I come in? she asked. Of course, I said, would you like some coffee? I'd rather just kiss you everywhere, she said. I told her that was fine by me. We could always drink the coffee later. But afterwards I realised that of course I didn't have any coffee. It was something I had said without thinking, in a kind of fog of the mind. The disappointments, the defeats. They never end.

The forecast was interrupted by an old recording of Hot Club de Norvège. The weather man broke down laughing just as he was about to explain that an area of low pressure was on its way in over the North. Sinking to his knees, he looked into the camera and asked the viewers if they really understood what kind of a society they were part of. Interrupted by his own laughter, he got no further before Hot Club had launched into a fine rendition of "Alabamy Bound."

Just as I got on the bus and was about to pay, the driver asked me how I was. I'm fine, thanks, I said and smiled. I put the money on top of the little ticket machine and he pushed the coins down into their respective slots. Surely that's not true, he said. Probably not, I replied and started moving down the bus. You're not seeing the bigger picture! the driver shouted behind me. I turned around and went back and leaned over him. That thing about a "bigger picture" is just something you've read, I said. He looked down and admitted that this was true. I gave him a quick slap across the cheek and looked back at the other passengers. Most of them nodded approvingly, some smiled and all the way at the back someone was clapping. Maybe this will teach you for next time, I said to the driver. He replied, but his voice was so soft that I couldn't understand what he said.

First I urinated in the bucket. Then I opened the door slightly and balanced the bucket on top of it, leaning it gently against the wall, so that it would fall if the door was opened. Then I shouted for Flügger. He was standing out in the library and I had to shout loudly for him to hear me. What is it? he shouted back. Come in here! I said. A few seconds later I could hear his footsteps getting closer. My heart started beating faster and I backed into the room. What is it? asked Flügger again. Come in here, I said. I could see him now. He moved slowly right up to the door and then he stopped. I worried that he would see the bucket, but he kept looking at the floor. I've been thinking about something, he said. Ok, but why don't you come in here? I said quickly. Flügger looked at me through the narrow opening. He hesitated, ran his fingers across his forehead and said: I don't think I believe in intimacy anymore. Never mind that, I said. Come in here, it will be easier to talk. I was starting to fear that he would smell the urine. Instead, he sank to his knees. I don't know what to do, he whispered, and it sounded like he was about to cry. It will be alright, I said. Do you think so? he said and looked up. What? I said. It's really difficult to hear what you're saying when you're out there in the hall. Flügger got up. I'm sorry, he said. It's just that I'm so afraid. He opened the door. The bucket fell perfectly.

One morning I woke up and knew that I wanted to run. But after getting dressed and having a quick look round the house, the desire was suddenly gone. I sat down in a chair and stared at the floor and waited for something to happen. After a while I began to cry. Slowly everything became difficult.

There was a flower on the window sill. Is it yours? I asked. Come here, she said. I went into the kitchen, but it was empty. Where are you? I asked. In here, her voice said from one of the cupboards. I opened the door and there she was, crammed in under the sink. Quick, get in, she said. I didn't think I'd fit at first, there was so little space, but once I was inside, there was more room than you'd think. It looks so small from outside, I said. She bent her fingers around the cupboard door and sort of heaved it in so that it shut again. It was completely dark. It smelled of dust and old food. We were huddled together very close. I could feel her breath on my face and it was warm. The important thing now is that we sit very, very still, she whispered.

I forgot what I wanted to ask you, the headmaster said. That's your problem then, I replied. He sighed and looked up at the ceiling. I had some snot on my finger which I carefully flicked at him. It stuck to the bottom of his chin. He didn't notice. Imagine if all this had been different, he said quietly.

Renate sat and looked at me. She stirred her tea with a spoon. Erik says you've never slept with anyone, she said. That's true, I said. You can do it with me if you like, she said. No thanks, I said. I'd rather just wait until it happens on its own. It never happens on its own, she said. Well, it still feels strange to do it with you now just because you say we can, I said. Neither of us said anything more, and then I left.

Would you like a pastry? Aud asked. The lion didn't reply because it couldn't understand what she said. It probably can't understand what I'm saying, Aud thought. She took out her pocketknife and made a small incision in her finger before sticking her whole hand into the cage. See, you understood that, she said. And that was all she managed. That's how animals are. They are different.

I'm going to go now, she said. Wait! I said, and ran up to get the balloons. Look, I can also do this! I almost sang while I threw them up in the air and caught them again with delicate, swaying movements. That isn't enough, she said. Yes, yes! It *is* enough! I shouted back and waved a particularly nice, yellow balloon in front of her face. But she wasn't interested. Before, when I didn't have any of this, she said, it was kind of exciting. But now that it takes up so much time, it's really tiring. She walked to the door and opened it. You just need to get more into it! I shouted, letting a balloon go so that it so that it flew up, making a long farting sound. She shook her head and closed the door behind her. I swiftly grabbed my trumpet and ran to the balcony. It was my last chance.

We decided to go to the cinema. She wanted to see an Iranian film, whereas I wanted to see something that made me not think. Above all, I wanted to see something that made me cease to exist, but those movies are on so rarely and when they are, it's always some useless matinée showing that you can never make. So we went with the Iranian film. I'd taken a hipflask with me and during the film I sat there drinking and thinking about this and that. Afterwards, as we walked home, I slyly covered my ears every time Inger tried to say anything about the film.

I stroked her cheek and whispered that what we had was amazing, but that it was impossible to describe with words. She turned to me and replied: and yet, now that you've said it, it's gone. During the course of the night I tried to take it back, but it was too late. In the morning we shared out our things between us.

Do you know how to sell shoes? the man asked. But I am so in love with you, I said. At first, he didn't understand, but then he began to remember. After a while, we embraced. Things are going to happen very quickly now, he said. I was already naked, he still had his socks and underpants on.

It was a Saturday. I had gotten up late and gone down to the bakery to buy a couple of bread rolls, and had only eaten one and now the other one was sat drying on the window sill. It was sunny outside and the bread was getting drier and drier with every second. I stood there for a long time looking at it. I knew that the moment was coming, both for the roll and for me.

It's not so easy to talk to you, she said. How do you mean?
I said. I don't know, maybe you've not read enough books,
she said. Not enough books? What books? She got up and
walked over to the shelf and took out a fairly thick book called
something in English. Have you read this? she asked. I hadn't.
She suggested that I should try reading it and that we could
speak again afterwards. I went home and sat down with it,
but I couldn't even get through the foreword. It had difficult
words and I'm not even particularly good at English. After
half an hour I gave up and went to sleep. The next day I went
back to her with the book and threw it on the floor. I said if
she wouldn't take me the way I was, we might as well give it
up. She laughed and said that was fine with her. It's completely
unreasonable that you ask me to read books! I said. Nothing is
unreasonable, she said. I can ask of you what I want. If you don't
satisfy my needs, then we can't be together. But what about my
needs? I said. She smiled. I already satisfy your needs, she said.
I didn't know what to say to that, she was right. I stood there
in silence for a moment and then I said: I don't accept this.
Complain then, she said and closed the door.

I decided to think about only one thing at a time, no matter what happened. The first thing I thought about was shyness. The second thing I thought about was condensation. The third thing I thought about was that picture of Khrushchev where he's banging his shoe against the lectern. After that I don't remember anything.

Jørgen switched off the fuse and everything went black. Bodil felt her way forward searching for matches, to no avail. Let me help you, Jørgen said. He knew where the matches were and now he felt the warmth from her body even as she pulled away. Don't be afraid, he said.

She stuck her feet out and shouted for me to lick the soles of her shoes. She hadn't worn them outside or anything, so I did it for a bit and it was alright. But then she wanted me to take the whole stiletto into my mouth and suck on it. I said that even I had limits and that maybe we should calm down a little. Her face reddened and she turned away. Maybe we can go to the cinema? I asked. You really don't understand what this is about, she said. I got up and found the paper and started to look through it to see what was on, but soon my spirit left me and I then didn't feel like doing anything at all.

A cow stood out in the field. I felt beckoned and climbed over the fence and walked towards her. Hello there, I said. Hello yourself, said the cow. I stood and looked at it for a moment. It was pretty. You're pretty, I said. Thanks, said the cow. We got to talking and later in the afternoon she allowed me to milk her. It felt strange in the beginning, but she showed me how and I felt I was learning quickly. Later, I drank her milk and we sat down to look at the landscape around us. We could both feel how the day was going to end in something new, something neither of us had experienced before.

I was in Malmö with Vegar. I had arrived the night before and slept in Vegar's expensive Hästens bed and now it was Sunday and we were out cycling around in the cool morning. I'm going to show you a gallery called Ping Pong, Vegar said. Ok, I said. We biked to Rådmansgatan and went down into a tiny basement room with white walls and three photographs of trees and grass. A young woman and a young man were there too. Vegar knew them. The woman was called Anna and the pictures on the walls were hers. I can't remember the man's name, but he seemed to be Anna's boyfriend. Anna was beautiful and my body trembled when I looked at her. Vegar noted that the trees in her pictures were bamboo and asked where she had taken them. She had been to Japan. I took the pictures in a Zen-Buddhist garden in Kyoto, she said. Then she said something else but I wasn't listening. I had already started taking my clothes off and was preparing myself for what I would say. No, Kim... Vegar said. Wait, I said. Anna looked at me and smiled. When I was completely naked, I stood in front of her and told her that I loved her. I love you too, she said. Her boyfriend jumped in and shouted, What are you doing? Can't you see that we're together? Are you an idiot? Yes, Bertil, or whatever your name is, I said, I am an idiot. Bertil sounds like a girl's name, by the way. It ends with –il, just like Bodil.

We sat at the table and looked at one another, she more seriously than I. After a moment she got up and went into the bedroom and fell face down on the mattress. I went after her and lay down beside her. She seemed to be crying. What is it? I asked. I'm so afraid of losing you, she said. I'm afraid of losing you too, I said. Then I added: but fear is the key. She looked up with teary eyes. What do you mean? she said. I'm only joking, I said. It's a book by Alistair Maclean.

I slid off the bed and started crawling underneath it. What are you doing? Signe asked. Wait for me here, I said and crawled in with the dark and the dust. It was harder to breathe under there, but it didn't take me long to find the outfit. Signe was lying above me and the bed creaked pleasingly. What are you trying to do? she asked again. Just wait, I said. She gave up and sighed. I thought we were going to make love, she said. Wait, I said again. I'd gotten the cape and hood on and was struggling with the leggings. What on earth are you doing? said Signe and stuck her head down under the bed. Don't look at me! I shouted. Ok, fine, she said and leaned back again. It's secret, I mumbled. The gloves were a bit stuck together and were difficult to get on, but I managed eventually. Right, if you don't come out now, I'm going, said Signe. I was now finally ready and I crawled out and stood over her. You can't tell anyone, but it is I who is 'Autumn-Man.' This is my secret identity. Signe gasped, she sat up and looked scared. But I wasn't worried, I knew Signe. She'd keep quiet. The fight could go on, this town would once again be a safe place to live.

You're so beautiful, I said. But that's not important, she said. Of course not, I said. I don't think you're so handsome, but I really like you as a person, she said. That's a nice thing to say, I said. Arne is handsome, she said. Do you remember him? He's really incredibly beautiful. He must be one of the best looking people I've ever met, she said. Yes, I said. He is quite handsome, that's true. People are complicated, she said. They have different qualities.

What if we slept next to each other, I said. Grete looked at me. How would that work? she said. We lie down and go to sleep, I said. Don't you think we'd start touching each other if we're lying so close? she said. But you don't want to do that, I said. No, but now it seems as if you're trying to get me to want to, she said. My serious face fell apart and I decided to admit everything, about how I'd lied when I said I only wanted to be friends; about how often I tried to stand as close to her as possible without her noticing; about how every time she called I tried to hide how happy it made me, and about how I had no interest in horses what so ever. She laughed and put her hand on my shoulder. You're so simple, she said. Then she got up and walked out. I stayed put, convinced that she'd be back with the flowers she'd gone out to buy and that she would tell me how relieved she was that we could finally show each other how we really felt. But she didn't come back. Not that evening or the next one or any evening after that. I tried to call, but she just hung up when she heard who it was. Towards the end of September I saw her in the street with Fredrik. They had a basketball between them and Grete was smiling. I hid behind a phone box, they didn't see me.

You're also alone, Jakob said. Irene sat across from him, knitting. I'm alone with you, she said. It might appear that way, Jakob said, but really you're just alone. Irene put the knitting down. How do you mean? she asked. Oh come on, Jakob said. We're all alone inside ourselves, everyone knows that. Irene looked at him. But I don't want to be alone, she said. I want to be with you. Jakob got up. Well, there's nothing I can do about that, he said. Do you want to take a bath? I'll scrub your back if you like. Irene looked down. I don't want to be alone, she said.

Please sit, Arntzen said. I sat down and took some papers out of my bag. Arntzen was getting a large binder down from a high shelf. It's nice here, I said. It's alright, he said. There was a knock on the door and a middle-aged woman stuck her head in. She looked at me and nodded and then she looked at Arntzen. Do you have a moment? she said. Arntzen excused himself and went out into the corridor with her. The woman started whispering but Arntzen had only half closed the door and I could hear what she was saying. Movement is always relative to something else, she said. You can't talk about something moving on it's own. I know that, Arntzen said, but I'm in the middle of a meeting, can we not do this later? The Universe is expanding, the woman said, slightly louder now. I got up and opened the door. I can go and come back another time, I said. Arntzen's face lit up. Are you sure? he said. Of course, I said. No problem. Thank you, the woman said. While she and Arntzen continued their conversation I walked down the corridor and sat down on the steps outside. It was still quite cold, but you could definitely feel that Spring was coming on. I remembered that it was my turn to shop, so I got out a piece of paper and made a list of things I would otherwise forget.

This is dangerous, she said. Not as long as neither one of us falls in love, I said. If neither of us falls in love then what's the point? she said. If you fall in love with me, I won't be able to see you any more, I said. Maybe I'll lie about it, she said. I'd be able to see it on you, I said. Are you sure? she said. I don't know, try. She looked at me and her face became serious. I have never met anyone like you, she said. There's something in me when we are together that makes me feel afraid and happy at the same time. I think we both love one another but that we're scared to admit it. She looked down. That was rubbish, I said. It wasn't hard to see through at all. She looked up at me and smiled. You try it, she said.

One morning I woke up completely of my own accord. There is opportunity here, I thought.

Trees don't die of old age. Their cells can split and regenerate without limit. As the tree becomes taller, the trunk gets thicker, so that it's always able to carry itself. You're not even able to carry this old suitcase, let alone get it onto this train about to leave for Hamburg. Your back hurts when you lift and your breathing is heavy. In a few years you'll be gone.

At night, if it's late enough, you can hear a sound in the trees that sounds like radio.

From the window in the bus which went from the airport into town, we could see writing painted in white on a billboard. What does it say? I asked. My father strained to read it as we drove past. 'The... best battle... is lost... love,' he read out loud. Is that what it said? I asked. That's what it looked like to me, he said.

Inger and Kjartan and I sat on a small hill drinking beer. We sort of know who each one of us are, but we can't know if we really know each other, Inger said. I didn't know what to say to that, I don't like it when people say such things and I wished she hadn't. Kjartan suddenly remembered something he had to do, it was important and he left. I stayed, alone now with Inger, silent and afraid. The sun was low in the sky, hiding behind a cloud, but you could see that it was there. This is so exciting, said Inger.

I'd gone to the park and sat on a bench when a horse came by. It asked if it could sit down and I said yes. We sat in silence for a while and then the horse took out a packet of cigarettes. I asked if I could have one, and I could. After a while I asked the horse if it lived nearby or what. I don't mean to be rude, said the horse, but I really don't feel like talking. It had sad eyes. No worries, I said. I turned away a little and looked up at the houses and trees that surrounded us. The horse sighed quietly. We sat like this and smoked until each had finished. Then the horse got up and said thanks. It's me who should be thanking you, I said. Ah, well, the horse said and went on its way. It had begun to cloud over and it looked like it was going to rain. It suddenly struck me how the horse had been completely naked while I had been fully dressed, and that neither of us had said anything about that. There is something in this, I thought, and I got up and took off my coat. It felt good. I took off my shoes and my socks. Then my trousers, jumper, t-shirt and underwear. It was cold, I had goose bumps, but I sat back down and bunched my clothes up next to me. Damn it, I said, aloud to myself as the first raindrop hit. People had started turning on the lights in their apartments. I thought that I should have brought coffee. I was freezing. I missed Ingeborg. I was no horse.

She stretched out on the bed. I've bought a new record, she said. Do you want to hear it? Sure, I said. She got up and went over to the record player. I don't think anyone has heard it before, she said. It's almost completely silent.

I clean the dining table and the bed and the floor in the bedroom and the floor in the hall and the floor in the living room, the floor in the shower. I clean the the toilet and the toilet bowl and the inside of the cupboard and the bath tub and the curtain rod and the taps, I wash the soap. I wash the cups and plates and knives and forks and pipes and drain. I wash the bin before I empty it and then I recycle the bottles and vacuum the rooms and the walls and the curtains. I clean the windows and polish the hinges and your breasts until they shine, but it's late, you say, and you have to go. Bye, maybe I'll see you tomorrow.

Kim? the man said. Yes, I replied. It's nothing, I'm just messing with you, he said. We sat in silence for a moment. Kim? the man said again. What do you want? I asked. He didn't reply, he just looked at me and smiled. What do you want? I said again. I'm still messing with you, he said. I'll stop now.

On the corner of Kirkegata and Revierstredet, on an electricity box, someone has written 'This is what I was afraid of the whole time', in green felt pen.

It's the most complicated part of the equation, but Susanne can't concentrate any more. She's too hungry. The numbers in her mind are constantly being pushed away by thoughts of fresh bread and cheese. She sighs and gets up and goes to the kitchen. She takes out some rice from the day before and some cottage cheese. She puts the kettle on to make tea. She leafs through the paper, reading bits here and there and what she reads makes her glum. The water boils and she sits down and begins to eat. While she eats, she thinks about what she's done during the day and what she will be doing tomorrow. One of her shoulders hurts and reminds her that she needs a higher chair. Slowly, the equation returns. As soon as she's finished eating, she goes back to it. She's sated now, ready for maths.

There's no real difference between people. The idea that we think we love one person more than another is a kind of misunderstanding, she said. Ok, but what about us? I said. There is no us, she said, or them. There's only we. Ok, I said, what about we? She stopped. Her face lit up, her arms shot into the air and then she shouted WE'RE FUMBLING IN THE DARK! and jumped as high as she could. People turned around to see who she was. They didn't understand that you can't see who someone is just by looking at them.

This is how: the days move at a speed where we only just notice that they're there, and most of the time we don't. Every now and then one may seem longer than another, but it makes no difference: when it's gone, it's gone. This is what we have. Regardless, I decide to spend my time trying to be better than you. Even if it makes me afraid and often costs a lot of money.

Are you hungry? she asked. Maybe, I said. She had some soup from the day before that she warmed up and then we sat down to eat it. She asked me what I had been doing and I told her about that. I asked her what she had been doing and she told me about that. Then none of us said anything and we just ate. From time to time I looked at her and wondered what she thought about things. I think she looked at me when she thought I didn't notice. When we were done eating, she asked if I wanted coffee. I said no and that I thought I should probably be going home. She nodded and then we didn't say anything more and then I left.

Hanne looked at me. She put her hands on my shoulders. I want it to be absolutely clear what this is about, she said. Do you think you could just write it down on a piece of paper? I said.

ABOUT THE AUTHOR

Kim Hiorthøy was born in Trondheim in 1973 and has worked as an illustrator, graphic designer, musician and cinematographer. 'You can't betray your best friend and learn to sing at the same time' is his debut novel, originally published in Norwegian by Oktober in 2002 and recently re-issued, to critical acclaim.

His first feature film, 'The Rules for Everything,' will be released in Norway early in 2017.

ABOUT NORDISK BOOKS

Nordisk Books was founded in Islington in 2016 with a view to increasing the amount of Scandinavian literary fiction available in the UK. With an abundance of crime thrillers from the Northern European peninsula having made it into translation, it seemed there was a gap as regards modern and contemporary non-genre literature. 'You can't betray your best friend and learn to sing at the same time' is Nordisk Books' second title after the key Danish work, Havoc, by Tom Kristensen.

Keep up with news and future releases by following us @nordiskbooks or by signing up to our newsletter on www.nordiskbooks.com